GH☺STBUSTERS™ II

Storybook by Jovial Bob Stine
Based on the screenplay by Harold Ramis and Dan Aykroyd
Based on the characters created by Dan Aykroyd and Harold Ramis.

SCHOLASTIC INC.
New York Toronto London Auckland Sydney

BILL MURRAY   DAN AYKROYD   SIGOURNEY WEAVER
HAROLD RAMIS   RICK MORANIS

An IVAN REITMAN Film

GHOSTBUSTERS II

COLUMBIA PICTURES Presents
"GHOSTBUSTERS II" · ERNIE HUDSON · ANNIE POTTS MUSIC BY RANDY EDELMAN
EXECUTIVE PRODUCERS BERNIE BRILLSTEIN · JOE MEDJUCK · MICHAEL C. GROSS BASED ON CHARACTERS CREATED BY DAN AYKROYD AND HAROLD RAMIS
DOLBY STEREO ® IN SELECTED THEATRES   WRITTEN BY HAROLD RAMIS AND DAN AYKROYD PRODUCED AND DIRECTED BY IVAN REITMAN   A COLUMBIA PICTURES RELEASE
© 1989 COLUMBIA PICTURES INDUSTRIES, INC. ALL RIGHTS RESERVED   Columbia Pictures
ORIGINAL SOUNDTRACK ALBUM AVAILABLE ON MCA RECORDS AND CASSETTES

Art direction and book design by David Tommasino

ISBN 0-590-42907-8

Copyright © 1989 by Columbia Pictures Industries, Inc.

All rights reserved. Published by Scholastic Inc.

12 11 10 9 8 7 6 5 4 3 2 1   9/8 0 1 2 3 4/9

Printed in the U.S.A.   34

First Scholastic printing, September 1989

INTRODUCTION

The ghosts were back. The supernatural was about to invade Dana Barrett's life again. But Dana didn't know it — until the afternoon her baby buggy took off by itself!

Tall, slender, chicly dressed Dana didn't feel terribly chic as she tried to carry two full bags of groceries while pushing the carriage containing her nine-month-old son, Oscar. She stopped at the door to her apartment building, juggled the heavy bags, and tried to dig her keys out of her purse.

"Frank, do you think you could give me a hand with these bags?" she called to the lazy building superintendent, who was leaning against the building watching her struggle.

"Okay, okay. It's not my job, but I'll do you a favor," Frank grumbled.

Dana set the brake on the baby carriage, handed the grocery bags to Frank, and continued to search for her keys. She didn't notice that the baby carriage had begun to vibrate.

Inside the carriage, Oscar gurgled with delight at the sudden movement. The carriage brakes seemed to unlock themselves. And then the carriage began to roll.

Dana reached for the handlebar — and realized that the carriage was rolling away from her! Faster and faster, the carriage rolled, as if pushed by an invisible hand.

Dana chased it down the sidewalk, running at full speed. "Help me! Somebody help me!" she frantically called as the buggy swerved down the crowded sidewalk — and off the curb.

The baby carriage bounced into a crosswalk, into the path of a speeding bus! Suddenly, it came to a dead stop, as if somebody had put on the brakes. The bus swerved by, missing the carriage by inches.

Dana ran into the street, picked up Oscar, and hugged him tightly. Something strange is happening, she thought.

CHAPTER 1

Things just weren't the same since the Ghostbusters had split up. This is what Ray Stantz was thinking as he pulled the Ectomobile up to the fashionable New York City brownstone. He and his partner Winston Zeddemore, wearing their official Ghostbusters uniforms, jumped out of the old ambulance, shouldering their proton packs.

A woman greeted them anxiously at the door. "How many are there, ma'am?" Ray asked.

"Fourteen. I hope you can handle them," the woman said. "It's been like a nightmare." She led them into the living room where the two former Ghostbusters faced . . . fourteen screaming kids! It was a birthday party, and Ray and Winston were the entertainment.

"Ghostbusters! Booo!" the kids yelled. "I thought we were having He-Man!"

After the party, Ray and Winston collected their small pay and slumped back out to *Ecto 1*. "That's it, Ray. It's over," Winston said sadly. "Ghostbusters doesn't exist anymore. In a year, these kids won't even remember who we are."

"After all we did for this city," Ray said, shaking his head. He tried to start up *Ecto 1A*. But the engine clanked and clunked and then died, as dead as the once-famous Ghostbusters company.

* * *

Across town in the studios of WKRR-TV, Dr. Peter Venkman, another former Ghostbuster, was just finishing up his weekly TV show, "The World of the Psychic."

"I predict that the world will end at midnight on New Year's Eve," one of Venkman's guests was saying.

"I think my other guest may disagree with you," Venkman told him, turning to the woman on his right. "Elaine?"

"According to my sources, the world will end on February 14, 2016," Elaine told Venkman.

"Valentine's Day! What a bummer!" Venkman declared. His ghostbusting days were over, but he still had the twinkle in his eye, still had the mischievous sense of humor. "Where did you get that date, Elaine?" he asked.

"I received this information from an alien in a Holiday Inn, in Paramus, New Jersey," Elaine replied.

After a few more questions, Venkman ended his show. "Next week we'll be discussing hairless pets," he told the viewers, holding up a hairless cat.

A few minutes later, he was wearily leaving the TV studio when he saw the mayor and a bunch of city officials in the hallway. "Hey — Lenny!" Venkman called to the mayor.

The mayor made a face and pretended not to know him. "Lenny — it's me — Peter!" Venkman called.

The mayor's assistant, Jack Hardemeyer stepped in Venkman's way. "Look — you stay away from the mayor," Hardemeyer said, glaring coldly at Venkman. "He wants to be elected governor. And we don't want him to be seen with frauds like you and your pals. You read me?"

"Okay," Venkman said, pretending to pout. "But because of you, I'm not voting for him!"

* * *

The next day, Dana Barrett went to her job at the Manhattan Museum of Art, where she restored famous old paintings. The head of the department, a strange young man named Janosz Poha, was busily working on an enormous oil portrait of Vigo the Carpathian, a cruel sixteenth-century king.

"You are doing very good work here," Janosz told Dana. "Soon you will be able to assist me with the important paintings."

"I've learned a lot here," Dana said. "But now that my baby is a little older, I'm thinking of rejoining the orchestra."

At the mention of Dana's baby, the figure on the large painting came to life. Vigo the Carpathian turned his head and stared at Dana. Neither of the two people in the gallery noticed the figure in the painting move.

Dana worked a while longer, but she was still troubled by the strange incident with the baby carriage the day before. She turned down Janosz's invitation to lunch, and hurried across the quad to see someone who might be able to help her — former Ghostbuster, Egon Spengler.

A brilliant research scientist, Spengler was in the middle of an experiment when Dana arrived. "Egon, what are you doing with these people?" she asked, seeing a large group of uncomfortable-looking people on the other side of a glass window.

"I'm trying to determine whether human

emotional states have an effect on the psychomagnetheric energy field," Spengler told her. "Stantz and I were working on it when we had to break up the Ghostbusters. We've kept these people waiting for two hours, and we've gradually increased the room temperature to ninety-five degrees. Now my assistant is going to ask them if they'd mind waiting another half hour."

As Spengler measured the angry reaction of the crowd of people, Dana told him what had happened to her baby carriage. "Hmm . . . I'd like to bring Ray in on your case," Spengler said thoughtfully.

"Okay," Dana agreed. "But not Venkman. We didn't part on very good terms. And we sort of lost track of each other when I got married." Dana paused and looked away. It was obvious that she still had some feeling for Venkman, even though she was trying to hide it. "I thought of calling Venkman after my marriage ended. But . . . anyway . . ."

She handed Spengler her card. "Here's my address and phone number. Will you call me?" Spengler nodded his head yes. "I'd rather you didn't mention any of this to Venkman, if you don't mind."

"I won't," Spengler told her. As he watched her leave, he wondered if ghostly forces really were responsible for the baby carriage's mysterious trip. And he began to wonder if it might not be time to call the Ghostbusters back together.

CHAPTER 2

Spengler and Stantz were at Stantz's small bookstore, about to go to Dana's apartment when Venkman burst in. "Where are you going?" he asked.

"Oh, just checking something for an old friend," Stantz told him.

"Who?"

"Who? Oh . . . just someone we know."

"Who, Ray?" Venkman demanded. He grabbed both of Stantz's ears and started to pull.

"Dana! Dana Barrett!" Stantz cried in pain.

Venkman smiled. There was *no way* he was going to miss out on this adventure!

A few minutes later, Dana was opening her apartment door to them. She saw Ray and Egon first and greeted them both warmly. She was about to close the door when Venkman appeared. Dana's mouth dropped open in surprise.

"I knew you'd come crawling back to me," Venkman said.

She glared at him coolly. "Hello, Peter," she said, without any emotion at all.

"I can see you're still very bitter about us," Venkman said. "But in the interest of science, I'm going to give it my best shot. Let's go to work, boys."

The three men began investigating the

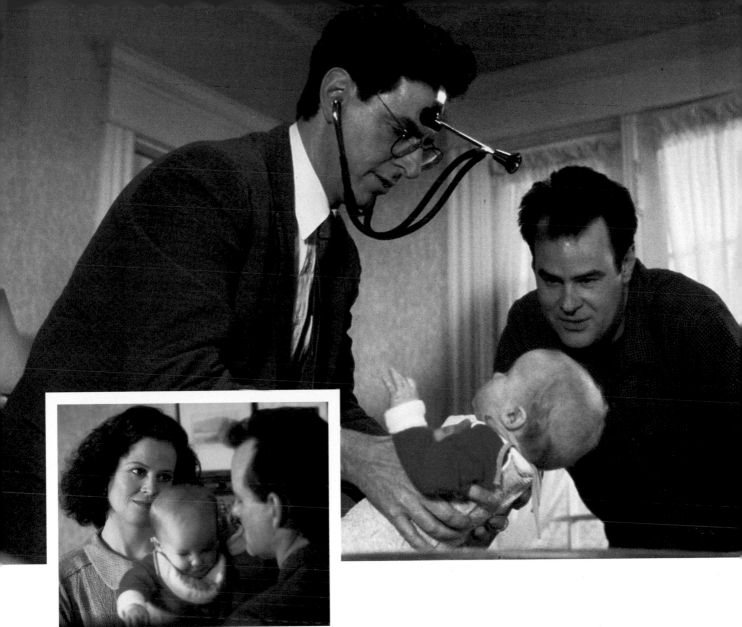

apartment and the baby. Spengler took a complete set of little Oscar's body and head measurements. "What are you going to do, Egon? Knit him a snowsuit?" Venkman asked.

Venkman picked up the baby and began clowning around with him. He pressed his nose into the baby's belly and pretended the baby was attacking him. "Help! Get him off quickly! He's gone completely berserk!"

Even Dana had to laugh at Venkman's hilarious antics. Then she remembered why they were there, and turned serious. "What do you think?" she asked.

"There's no doubt about it. He's got his father's looks," Venkman said. "The kid is ugly. Extremely ugly. And smelly."

"This is serious," Dana insisted. "I need to know if anything is wrong with my baby."

The three Ghostbusters could find nothing wrong. "I think we should see if we can find anything abnormal on the street," Spengler suggested.

"Finding something abnormal on the street in New York City shouldn't be too hard!" Venkman exclaimed.

A few minutes later, Dana was walking down the street with Venkman, retracing the path of the runaway carriage. Stantz and Spengler trailed behind, measuring PKE valences with their highly sensitive equipment.

"That's where the buggy stopped," Dana said suddenly, stopping short and pointing.

"Okay. Let's take a look," Venkman said. He stepped right into the street, paying no attention to the cars honking and whizzing past. He began motioning like a traffic cop and brought all the cars to a stop.

Stantz and Spengler stepped into the street, reading their PKE meters. "Nothing. Not a trace," Stantz said, shaking his head.

"Why don't we try the giga-meter?" Spengler suggested.

"What's that?" Venkman asked.

"It's a new gauge to measure psychomag-netheric energy in G.E.V.'s — giga electron volts," Stantz explained.

"That's a thousand million electron volts," Spengler added.

"I knew that," Venkman insisted.

Spengler switched on the giga-meter, passed it over the spot on the street where the buggy stopped — and the meter zoomed into the red zone. The device started clicking wildly.

"I think we hit the honey pot, boys," Stantz declared, staring at the meter. "There's something brewing under the street!"

* * *

That evening at the Manhattan Museum of Art, Janosz Poha was working late on the painting of Vigo. The museum was closed and silent. The only sound was the scrape of Janosz's brush as he worked on the old painting.

Janosz didn't notice as the eyes of Vigo started to glow. The artist touched his brush to the canvas, and a powerful current of red, crackling energy surged through the brush.

Janosz cried out as the energy force encircled his body, bringing unbearable pain to every part of him.

The figure of Vigo moved in the painting. His eyes glowed menacingly as he came to life. He called out to the helpless Janosz in a deep, commanding voice. "I, Vigo, the scourge of Carpathia, the sorrow of Moldavia, command you!" he cried.

"Command me, lord," Janosz cried, bowing before the painting.

"On a mountain of skulls in a castle of pain, I sat on a throne of blood!" Vigo declared, his voice booming in the large gallery. "What was will be; what is, will be no more. Now is the season of evil. Find me a child that I might live again!"

Bolts of crackling, red energy shot from Vigo's eyes into Janosz's eyes. Janosz screamed and fell to his knees.

CHAPTER 3

The Ghostbusters had been ordered by a judge to stop all ghostbusting activities. But this was too big to ignore. Something strange was going on under East 77th Street, and they *had* to find out what it was.

That night, surrounded by official-looking safety cones and reflectors, and wearing official-looking hardhats, Spengler began jackhammering the street. The noise was so loud, he didn't even notice when a police patrol car pulled up.

"How ya doin'?" a curious cop called out.

"Fine. It's cutting fine now," Spengler said, trying not to look guilty.

"*Why* are you cutting?" the cop asked.

"Why are we cutting? Uh . . . " Spengler was stuck for an answer. "Uh . . . *boss*!"

Luckily, Venkman and Stantz came walking up, wearing hardhats and work uniforms. "What does it *look* like we're doing?" Venkman asked, pretending to be angry. "We're killing ourselves here because someone downtown has nothin' better to do than to make us work late on a Friday night!"

The answer seemed to satisfy the policeman. Spengler breathed a sigh of relief as the patrol car drove away, and they continued jackhammering.

After a while, deep down in the street, the jackhammer hit metal. They cleared away the rubble to find an old, iron manhole cover. "NYPRR?" Stantz asked, reading the letters on the old manhole cover. "What can that be? Help me lift this."

Using crowbars, they pried open the metal cover. Then Stantz beamed a flashlight into the deep, dark hole below. "It's an old air-shaft," he told his companions. "It just goes on forever."

The reading on the giga-meter was very high. "We need a deeper reading. Somebody has to go down there," Spengler said. He and Venkman stared at Stantz.

"Thanks, boys," Stantz said, resigned to his fate.

As the traffic swerved around them, they snapped Stantz into a harness, and lowered him into the hole on a strong cable. Stantz descended deeper and deeper into the musty airshaft. At the bottom of the shaft, he swung free, finding himself in an enormous tunnel of some kind.

Pulling out a flashlight, he beamed it all around him. He could make out polished tile walls, colorful tile mosaics. A large tile sign read: VAN HORNE STATION.

Suddenly, Stantz knew where he was. He was inside an old station of the New York Pneumatic Railroad. The railway was an experimental subway station built around 1870. Air-powered trains were blown back and forth in the tunnels by gigantic fans.

Stantz pulled out his walkie-talkie and excitedly told his partners what he had found. "What's the meter reading?" Spengler, always with his mind on business, wanted to know.

Stantz had to whistle when he saw the meter results. "Off the top of the scale!" he reported up to them. "This place is really hot. Lower me to the floor."

Up on the street, Venkman and Spengler fed Stantz more cable. Down he went, into the old station. "Hold it! Stop! Whoa!" he suddenly screamed into his walkie-talkie.

Below him, his flashlight revealed a river of glowing bubbling, seething slime. Stantz could hear all the sounds of the city down there: the rumble of the subway, engines throbbing, steam hissing, water rushing, the roar of traffic, the cry of human voices. And below him, the bubbling river of slime gurgled and oozed.

Despite his horror, Stantz remembered that he was a scientist. He unhooked a device on his utility belt, shot a long scoop into the disgusting slime, and brought up a sample of it.

He almost had the sample tucked away when a bony arm with long, skeletal fingers reached up out of the slime and grabbed at his feet!

Stantz jerked up his legs and the hand just barely missed him. Several more arms poked up from the slime and tried to grab him.

"Haul me up, Venkman! *Now!*" he cried.

But up on the street, his two companions had their own problems. A Con Edison power company supervisor had pulled up and didn't look very happy about the hole that had been dug. "Okay, what's the story here?" he demanded.

Venkman tried to bluff him the way he had bluffed the policeman. "What, I got time for this? We've got three thousand phones out in the Village, and about eight million miles of cable to check!"

The supervisor was not buying it. "The phone lines are over there," he said, pointing to the curb.

Venkman slapped Spengler on the head. "I *told* ya!"

Meanwhile, Stantz's panicked voice came sputtering up through the walkie-talkie. "Help! Pull me up! It's alive! It's eating my boots!!"

Up on the street, the policeman had returned. Venkman switched off the walkie-talkie, cutting off Stantz's terrified screams. "You ain't with Con Ed *or* the phone company," the policeman said. "We checked. Tell

me another one."

Venkman thought hard. "Gas leak?" he tried.

"Get me out of here!" Stantz was screaming down below. He was halfway up the airshaft, and the bubbling slime was following him up. He frantically began kicking at the wall. A hard kick broke through an old electrical power line.

Venkman and the others saw a flash of light down in the hole. They heard Stantz scream. Then one by one, all of the lights on the street went out. In a few seconds, the entire city had been plunged into darkness.

"Sorry," Stantz said quietly, down in the hole.

CHAPTER 4

The courtroom judge looked sour and unhappy to be there. The three Ghostbusters were in big trouble. The list of charges against them was a mile long! They were in even bigger trouble since their lawyer was Louis Tully, the nerdy little man they had saved from the clutches of Gozer, the Destructor in their last big adventure.

"I'm sure you'll be okay. You won't go to prison," Dana whispered to Venkman.

"Don't worry about me. I'm like a cat," Venkman told her.

"You mean you cough up hairballs all over the rug?" Dana asked.

"No. I always land on my feet," Venkman said.

"Good luck," Dana said, and gave him a quick, unexpected kiss.

The trial got underway. Jack Hardemeyer, the mayor's oily assistant, whispered to the judge that the mayor was eager to get the Ghostbusters behind bars.

"It shouldn't be hard to get them put away with *this* list of charges," the judge declared.

The trial was definitely stacked against the three Ghostbusters. After several hours, the

"Yes. What is it?" the judge asked irritably.

"Can I have some of your water?" Louis asked.

"Get on with it!" the judge screamed.

Looking very frightened, Louis began his final argument on behalf of the Ghostbusters. "Your Honor, I don't think it's fair to call my clients frauds. Okay, the blackout was a big problem for everyone. I was stuck in an elevator for about three hours, and I had to go to the bathroom the whole time. But I don't blame them, because once I turned into a dog and they helped me. Thank you."

Louis took his seat. The three Ghostbusters shook their heads sadly.

prosecutor called Venkman to the stand. "Dr. Venkman, why were you digging the hole in the street?"

"There are things in this world that go way beyond human understanding," Venkman began. "Things that can't be explained and that most people don't want to know about anyway." He pointed to the jar of slime on the evidence table, the slime that Stantz had pulled out of the hole. "That's where the Ghostbusters come in."

Sneering skeptically, the judge called upon Louis to make his final arguments. "Your Honor, may I approach the bench?" Louis asked nervously.

"That was the worst presentation of a case I've ever heard in a court of law!" the judge cried. "I find these three men guilty on all counts! I order you to pay fines of twenty-five thousand dollars each, and I sentence you to eighteen months in prison!"

The courtroom was in an uproar. Stantz quietly poked Venkman in the ribs. "Uh-oh. She's twitching," he whispered.

They both looked over at the jar of slime on the evidence table. "Duck," Stantz whispered, and the three Ghostbusters hit the floor.

There was a loud rumbling. The jar began to shake. And then two enormous, human-looking ghosts burst out of the jar!

They hovered menacingly over the judge. He recognized them immediately. "Oh, no! The Scoleri Brothers!" he cried in horror.

Ten feet tall, the Scoleri Brothers were strapped into crackling electric chairs. As the current hummed and sparked, they struggled to get free, to get at the judge.

So scared he could barely walk, the judge ducked down on the floor with the Ghostbusters. "You've got to do something!" he shouted. "I tried them for murder. They were electrocuted. Now they want to kill me!"

"Maybe they just want to appeal," Venkman cracked.

The ghostly Scoleri Brothers burst free from their electric chairs and began shooting high-voltage lightning from their fingers at the judge.

"You've got to stop them! Please!" the judge pleaded to the Ghostbusters.

"As their attorney, I'd have to advise them against it," Louis said, sounding very much

like a lawyer.

"All right! All right! You can all go free! You're all innocent! Case dismissed!" the judge cried. "Now do something!"

"Let's go to work, boys!" Stantz cried.

The three Ghostbusters rushed to the evidence table, picked up their proton packs, and quickly strapped them on. They flipped on the power switches and grabbed up their particle throwers. "All right, throwers. Set for full neutronas on stream!" Stantz instructed.

The Scoleri Brothers, crackling with high-voltage fury, were about to wipe out the poor, terrified judge. "Hey — why don't you pick on someone your own size!" Venkman screamed.

"Open 'em up — now!" Stantz cried, and the Ghostbusters' wands exploded with pow-

erful streams of energy. Working as a team, they pushed the Scoleris closer and closer to the traps Stantz had set on the floor.

The ghost brothers fought back, shooting bolts of lightning from their fingertips. But the Ghostbusters' proton streams were too powerful for them. A few seconds later, the ghosts were pushed into the traps, and the traps were snapped shut.

Venkman quickly checked the meters on the outside of the traps. "*Ocupado!*" he announced.

The judge, the spectators, and reporters slowly climbed to their feet. Flashbulbs began to pop as wide smiles spread across the faces of the three Ghostbusters.

"Case closed, boys!" Venkman declared happily. "We're back in business!"

CHAPTER 5

Reunited, the Ghostbusters were busy all over the city now, doing what they did best — trapping ghosts wherever they popped up.

One afternoon, Venkman came to see Dana at the studio where she worked in the Manhattan Museum. He entered quietly and sneaked up behind her. "So this is what you do?" he asked, looking at a priceless painting by Vermeer. "You're really good, you know."

"I didn't paint it. I'm just cleaning it!" Dana told him, laughing. "This painting is worth about ten million dollars."

Venkman squinted at the painting. "You know, you can go to Art World and get these huge, sofa-sized paintings for about forty-five bucks!"

Janosz suddenly entered, interrupting their conversation. Dana introduced them. "And what's that you're working on, Johnny?" Venkman asked, eyeing the oil painting of Vigo.

"It's a self-portrait of Prince Vigo," Janosz told Venkman. "He was a very powerful magician. A genius in many ways."

"And also a lunatic," Dana exclaimed. "I

hate this painting. I've felt very uncomfortable ever since they brought it up from storage."

"I know what it needs," Venkman said, enthusiastically picking up a paint brush. "A fluffy little white kitten in the corner!" He reached the brush toward the painting, but Janosz quickly pulled his hand back.

"I've got to be going," Venkman said. He waved good-bye to Dana and called, "Later, Johnny!" to Janosz.

As Dana returned to her workbench, the eyes of Vigo on the painting turned to follow her. Dana caught a glimpse of the movement. Curious, she stared at the painting. She started to walk back, then spun around quickly. This time she was sure she had seen the evil eyes move! Suddenly very frightened, she turned and ran from the studio.

* * *

Meanwhile, in the old firehouse that served as Ghostbusters Headquarters, Spengler and Stantz had made an astounding discovery about the slime they had taken from the old subway tunnel.

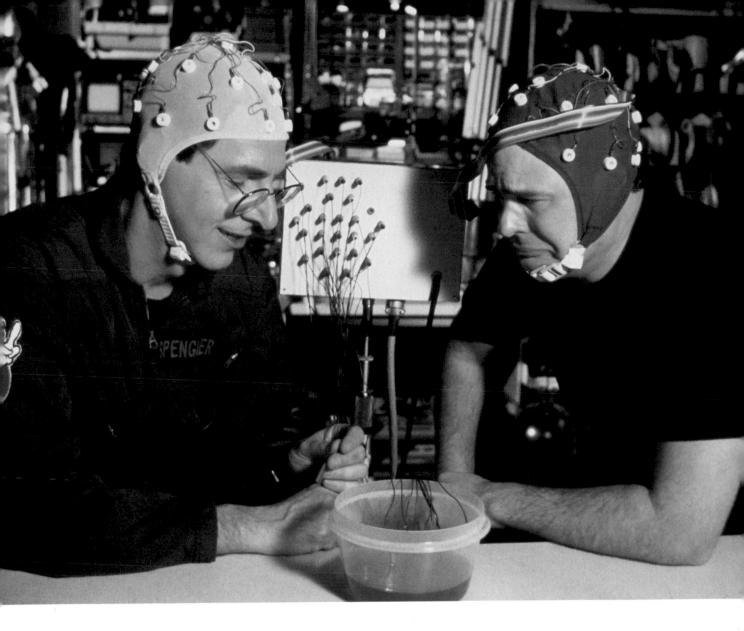

"Just look at this," Stantz told Venkman, removing the slime specimen from the freezer and popping it into the microwave. "We've been studying this stuff."

"And now you're going to eat it?!" Venkman exclaimed.

"Just watch," Stantz instructed. He leaned down and began shouting insults at the mysterious substance. "You worthless piece of slime! You ignorant disgusting blob!"

The slime bubbled and swelled with each insult. The more Stantz insulted it, the bigger it got. "It's remarkable," Stantz told Venkman. "It reacts to human emotions."

"We've found it at every ghost sighting we've been to lately," Spengler added.

"You mean this stuff actually feeds on bad vibes?" Venkman asked.

"Like a goat on garbage," Stantz replied.

"It gets bigger and nastier from insults, and you can calm it down by being nice to it," Stantz continued. "It likes soft music, songs like that old folk song, 'Kumbaya.' And it loves Jackie Wilson music. Watch this."

Spengler spooned some of the slime into an old toaster. Then Stantz clicked on a cassette player, and the Jackie Wilson song "Higher and Higher" blasted from the speakers. Immediately, the toaster began shaking, spinning, and moving in time with

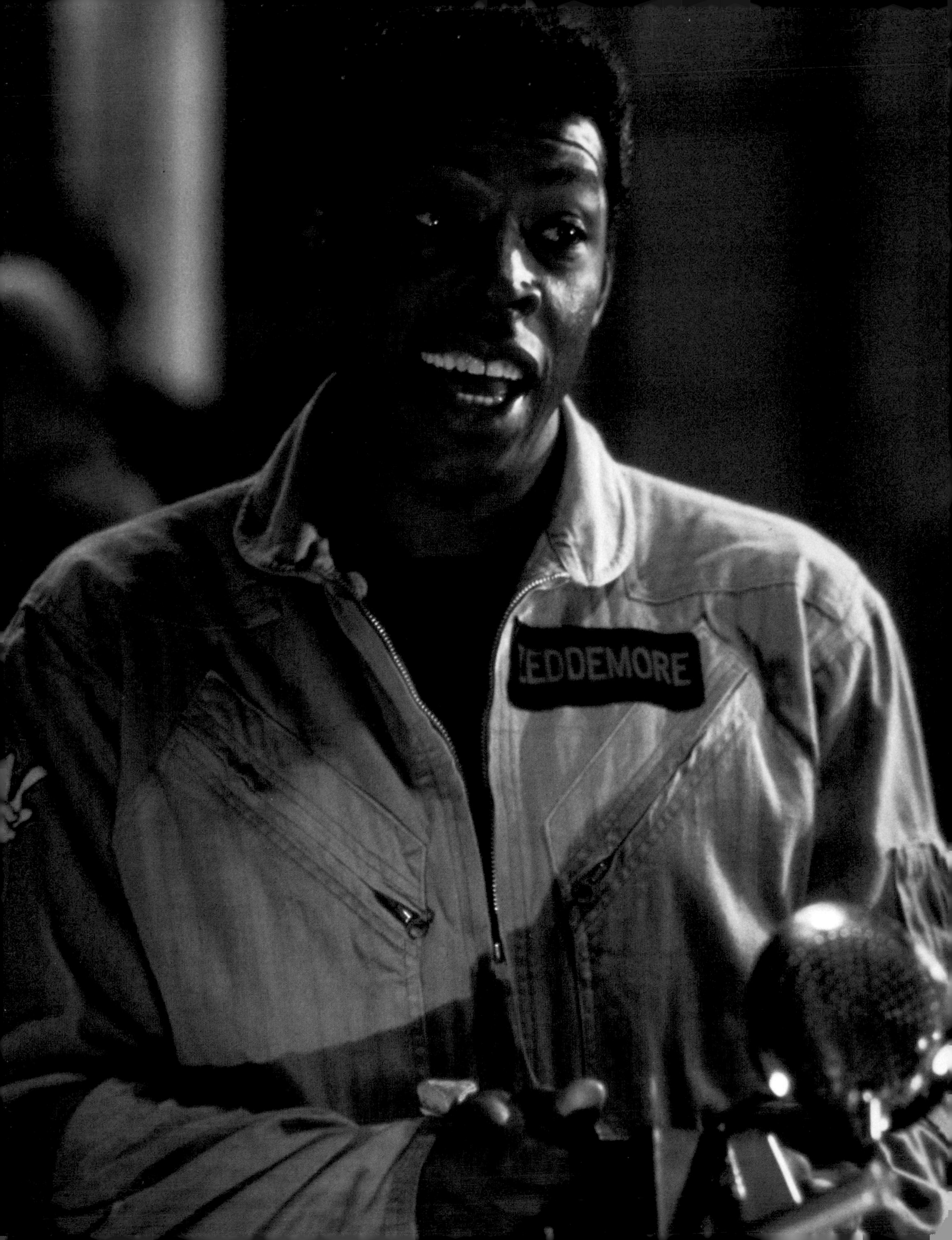
ZEDDEMORE

the music. Then it shot two pieces of toast into the air and caught them without missing a beat.

"Wow! This could be a major Christmas gift item!" Venkman declared.

"Right," Winston said, entering the lab. "And the first time someone gets mad, their toaster will eat their hand!"

* * *

That night in her apartment, Dana brought little Oscar into the bathroom to give him a bath. She turned on the faucets of the old claw-footed bathtub, checked the water temperature, then turned away to undress the baby.

Dana didn't see the water turn to pink slime as it poured into the tub. She turned off the faucets and went back to the baby. When she turned away, both taps began to spin by themselves. The whole tub began to flex and bulge. The rim of the tub puckered up like a big mouth.

Still not noticing anything unusual, Dana picked up Oscar and started to lower him into the bathtub. The tub began to close around the baby like a big mouth swallowing its dinner.

Dana screamed and pulled Oscar out of its grasp. Then she ran from the room as the bathtub convulsed, spewing up buckets of slime.

CHAPTER 6

Dana ran to Venkman's apartment with Oscar. Venkman called his partners and told them to investigate Dana's bathtub. The next morning, he met Stantz, Spengler, and Winston outside the museum.

"Find anything at Dana's?" Venkman asked.

"Nothing much," Stantz told him. "Just some mood-slime residue around the bathtub. But we *did* turn up some interesting information about this Vigo character you mentioned."

He went on to tell Venkman what they had learned. Vigo had lived for 105 years, and he hadn't died of old age. He was poisoned, stabbed, shot, hanged, stretched, and drawn and quartered. He was also known as Vigo the Cruel, Vigo the Torturer, and Vigo the Despised.

"This guy was a bad monkey," Stantz said. "Just before his head died, his last words were, 'Death is but a door, time is but a window. I'll be back.'"

"Quick — let's go upstairs and check out the painting," Venkman said.

They tricked the guard and hurried up to the studio. Janosz was working on the Vigo painting when the four Ghostbusters entered. He rushed over and stopped them at the door.

"Dr. Venkman? Dana is not here."

"I know," Venkman said.

"Then why have you come?"

"We got a major creep alert," Venkman told him, "and your name was first on the list."

Stantz turned to Spengler and Winston. "Let's sweep it, boys." They began scanning the studio with their detection equipment.

"What exactly are you looking for?" Janosz demanded, suddenly very nervous.

"We'll know when we find it," Venkman told him. He walked up to the painting of Vigo. "This is the one Dana said looked at her." He began shouting at the painting. "Hey, you — Vigie! Look at me. I'm talking to you. Hey! Look at me when I'm talking to you!"

But the eyes in the painting didn't budge.

"Okay. He's playing it cool," Venkman said. "Let's finish up our readings and get outta here."

Venkman walked off, leaving Stantz alone with the painting. Stantz scanned it with his giga-meter until his eyes met Vigo's. Suddenly a burning red ray shot from Vigo's eyes into Stantz's. Stantz stood there frozen, unable to look away, unable to move.

"Now that's one ugly dude," Winston said, coming up behind Stantz and breaking the spell. "Hey, you all right, Ray?"

"Yeah. I'm fine. I just got light-headed for a second there," Stantz replied. Trying to shake off the weird feeling, he followed his buddies out the door.

Stantz climbed behind the wheel of *Ecto 1A,* and the others piled in, not realizing that Stantz was still under Vigo's spell. They began to realize that something was wrong when Stantz began driving extremely fast, honking the horn at everyone, and swerving recklessly through traffic.

"Going a little fast, aren't we, Ray?" Winston asked.

"Are you telling me how to drive?" Stantz snarled viciously, and tromped down even harder on the accelerator. He barreled through a red light, sending pedestrians fleeing on both sides of the car.

"You're gonna kill somebody!" Winston screamed.

Stantz got a crazed look on his face. "No. I'm gonna kill *everybody!*"

He swerved off the road and aimed *Ecto 1A* at a big tree. Frantically trying to save their lives, Winston hit Stantz over the head, knocking him out. Then, reaching over Stantz, Winston grabbed the wheel and stomped on the brake.

The car skidded into the tree and stopped. The dazed Ghostbusters came tumbling out. "What happened?" Stantz asked. "It was the strangest thing. I knew what I was doing, but I couldn't stop. This terrible feeling just came over me. I just felt like driving into that tree and ending it all."

They inspected the damage to their vehicle. "Watch him, Egon," Venkman whispered to Spengler. "Keep a close watch on Stantz. Don't even let him shave."

* * *

At Ghostbusters Headquarters that evening, Louis Tully strapped on a proton pack and prepared to go after the mischievous, green ghost Slimer. "Okay, Stinky, this is it," he warned, even though Slimer was nowhere to be seen.

Louis strapped a rearview mirror to a headband and pulled it on. He was eager to prove that he could be a Ghostbuster, too. Capturing that smelly, junk-food-eating Sli-

mer would be a good start.

Sensing adventure, Slimer poked his head down through the ceiling and scanned the room. Louis spotted the ghost in his rearview mirror. "Okay, let's boogie!" he said quietly.

He whirled around and fired a proton stream at Slimer. "Whoops — missed." His shot sliced a burning gash across the ceiling.

Janine, the office secretary, entered the room and had to duck as a bolt of energy sliced across the room and hit the wall. Slimer, giggling, ducked out of sight.

"Oh, I'm sorry!" Louis cried.

"What are you doing up here?" Janine asked.

"Trying to get that smelly green thing," Louis told her, removing his rearview mirror. "The guys asked me to help out. I'm like the fifth Ghostbuster."

"Well, good night, Louis," Janine said. She turned and started to leave.

"Uh . . . Janine . . . do you feel like maybe getting something to eat on the way home?" Louis asked awkwardly.

"I'd like to," Janine said quickly, "but I promised Dr. Venkman I'd baby-sit for Oscar tonight. He and Dana are going out to dinner." Then Janine had an idea. "Do you want to baby-sit with me?"

Louis didn't have to think twice. He quickly agreed, and the two of them closed up and headed to Peter Venkman's apartment.

* * *

While Venkman was out on a date with Dana, his partners were far below the street, on an underground expedition for slime. Guided by a very old map, the three Ghost-busters found their way to Van Horne Sta-

tion. Crossing to the edge of the platform, they looked down at the river of slime.

"Let's find out how deep it is," Stantz said. He had a long, coiled rope with a weight on the end attached to his utility belt. He tossed it down into the middle of the slime and watched it sink. "Eight feet . . . nine feet . . . ten. . . ."

"Is the line sinking?" Winston asked.

"No. The slime is rising," Spengler realized.

Stantz looked down and saw the sticky, bubbling slime rising over the edge of the platform and around his boots. "Let's get out

of here, boys!" he screamed.

He tried to pull out the weighted line, but it was stuck. His buddies tried to help, but whatever was holding onto the line was stronger than all three of them!

Tugging desperately at the line, they were being pulled closer and closer to the edge of the platform. Stantz finally managed to unhook the belt. Spengler let go in time.

But Winston didn't. He was jerked off his feet and pulled down into the flowing slime.

Stantz and Spengler looked at each other, took a deep breath, and leaped in after him.

CHAPTER 7

Winston climbed out of the manhole first, followed by Stantz and Spengler. They were exhausted and covered with slime.

"Nice going, Ray. What were you trying to do — drown me?" Winston screamed angrily.

"It wasn't my fault you were too stupid to drop that line!"

"Watch your mouth man," Winston growled, "or I'll punch your lights out."

"If you two are looking for a fight," Spengler broke in, putting up his fists, "you've got one."

All three of them started to fight. Spengler was the first to come to his senses. He tried to pull them apart. "Strip! Right now! Get out of those clothes!"

They pulled off the slime-covered clothes and tossed them down the open manhole. Standing in their long underwear, they looked ridiculous — but they had returned to their normal personalities.

"We've got to tell Venkman!"

Running at top speed, they hurried to the fancy French restaurant where Venkman and Dana were having dinner. Forgetting that they were in their underwear, they swept past the maître d' and circled Venkman's table.

"I guess you guys didn't know about the dress code here," Venkman said. "It's really kind of a coat and tie place."

"It's a river of evil," Stantz said excitedly. "It's all over the city — well, under it, actually."

"Rivers of the stuff," Winston added.

"And it's all flowing to the museum!" Spengler added. He gestured excitedly and a glob of wet slime flew off his sleeve and landed on a well-dressed diner. "Sorry!" he called.

"Arrest these men!" the maître d' came running up to the table, followed by two policemen. The next thing the Ghostbusters knew, all four of them were out on the street.

"Look, we're not drunk and we're not crazy. This is a matter of vital importance," Spengler pleaded with the cops. "We've got to see the mayor."

It took a lot more begging and persuading, but soon the cops gave in. "Okay, we'll take you to the mayor. Follow us," one of them said.

Racing through the city streets at full speed, the Ghostbusters followed the patrol car to Gracie Mansion, the mayor's house. But would their warning be in time?

* * *

At the museum, Janosz stood before the painting as the terrible Vigo came to life. "I await the word of Vigo," Janosz said, completely under Vigo's spell.

"The season of evil begins tomorrow with the new year," Vigo bellowed. "Bring me the child, that I might live again."

Janosz bowed his head and made a request of his own. "Lord Vigo," he began, "the mother, Dana, is fine and strong. If I bring the baby . . . could I have the woman?"

"So be it," came the reply. "On this the day of darkness, she will be ours — wife to you and mother to me."

Janosz left quickly and hurried to do Vigo's bidding, to kidnap Dana and her child.

* * *

At Gracie Mansion, the Ghostbusters, now dressed in police raincoats, were trying to tell their incredible story to the mayor. But it was a bit too incredible. He just wasn't buying it.

"Mr. Mayor, there is a psychomagnetheric slime flow of immense proportions building up under this city," Stantz warned.

"Psycho-what??" the mayor cried. "Doesn't anybody speak English anymore?"

The mayor refused to hear any more about it. He went back to his dinner party. His assistant, Hardemeyer, came over quickly. "That's quite a story," he told the Ghostbusters. "Would you consider telling this slime thing to some people downtown?"

"Now you're talking!" Venkman said eagerly. "Let's go!"

Unfortunately, the people downtown were the doctors in the hospital psychiatric ward! Hardemeyer ordered the four trapped Ghostbusters locked into straitjackets. "The mayor wants them kept under strict observation for a few days," he told the psychiatrist.

* * *

Dana came home from the restaurant to find Louis and Janine sitting on the couch. As the evening wore on, all three of them waited to hear word about the Ghostbusters.

"I think I hear Oscar," Dana said. Tiptoeing into the baby's room, she saw to her horror that the crib was empty! The window was open. "Louis!" she called.

Louis and Janine came running in. Dana looked out the window. There was the baby, standing on the ledge fifty feet above the street, staring off into the distance.

In a panic, Dana managed to climb out onto the ledge. She inched her way closer and closer to the baby.

She stopped when she saw a ghost floating in mid-air. It looked like a sweet, kindly English nanny. It was pushing a carriage toward Oscar. As the ghost drew closer, Dana could see its face. It looked a lot like Janosz Poha.

Dana watched frozen in horror as the ghost picked up the baby and put him down in the carriage. The ghost turned and smiled at Dana, and the smile became a hideous grin. Shrieking wildly, the ghost took off. Oscar never made a sound.

Jumping back into the apartment, Dana told Louis to find Venkman. "Tell him what's happened!"

"Where are you going?" Louis asked.

"To the museum — to get my baby back!"

CHAPTER 8

At the psychiatric ward in the hospital, the Ghostbusters were not having any success convincing the psychiatrist to let them go.

"We think the spirit of Vigo the Carpathian is alive in a painting at the Manhattan Museum," Stantz explained.

"I see," said the psychiatrist, talking to Stantz as if he were a child. "And are there any other paintings in the museum with bad spirits in them?"

Meanwhile, at the museum, the powerful spirit of Vigo was everywhere. Dana rushed into the studio and saw her baby lying on a table in front of the awful painting. She picked Oscar up and hugged him tightly.

"I knew you would come," Janosz said, stepping out from behind the painting.

"What do you want with my baby?" Dana cried.

"He will be the vessel for the spirit of Vigo. You, Dana, will be the mother of the ruler of the world!"

"You're not taking my baby!" Dana cried. She started toward the door. But suddenly

Oscar floated out of her arms and flew back to the table in front of the painting. Dana stared in horror at the motionless figure of Vigo, realizing for the first time just how powerful he was.

* * *

As the last day of the year dawned, the Ghostbusters were still locked up in the psychiatric ward.

Meanwhile, all over the city strange things were happening. The fountain in front of the Plaza Hotel started to spout slime. Slime began pouring into the East River.

When a glob of the slime fell on a woman's mink coat, the minks came alive and attacked her!

The officers manning the phones at police headquarters were getting some very weird calls: " . . . Look lady, of course there are dead people there. It's a cemetery. Huh? They were asking you for directions??"

"What's that you say? The park bench was chasing you?"

"The *Titanic* just arrived at the pier??"

No one could explain these strange occurrences — and no one wanted to!

Except for the Ghostbusters. To their surprise, Louis managed to get them released. Louis' cousin Sherman, a skin doctor, signed the release papers — and the Ghostbusters were back in action — with little time to spare.

By the time they got to the museum, the entire building was covered by a thick shell of slime. Workmen and firemen tried to blast or dig their way through the slime, but they couldn't even make a dent.

The Ghostbusters strapped on their proton packs and readied their particle throwers. "Throw 'em!" Stantz instructed.

They began to spray the front doors of the building with bolts of proton energy — but even their weapons couldn't dent the impenetrable slime.

"Okay — who knows 'Kumbaya'?" Venkman asked the firemen. He lined up the confused firemen in front of the museum and started them singing the sweet folk song very gently. Before long, they were all holding hands and swaying to the music.

Stantz inspected the wall. The singing managed to open up only a tiny hole in the wall of slime. "It won't work," Spengler said sadly. "There's no way we can generate enough positive energy to crack that shell."

"I can't believe that things have gotten so bad in this city that there's no way back," Stantz exclaimed. "There've got to be a few sparks of sweet humanity left in this burned-out burg. We just have to mobilize it!"

"We need something that everyone can get behind," Spengler said. "Something good — "

"And pure," Venkman added.

"And decent," Winston added to that.
But what?

* * *

As crowds gathered to view the hideous,
bubbling slime that covered the museum, the
mayor and Hardemeyer pulled up in an official limo. "I've had it with you," Hardemeyer
screamed at Venkman. "Get back in that
clown car and get out of here!"

"I've got news for you," Venkman angrily
snapped back. "You've got Dracula's brother-
in-law in there, and he's got my girlfriend and
her kid. At midnight tonight, while you're at
your New Year's Eve party, he's going to come
to life and start doing amateur head

transplants!"

The mayor turned wearily to Venkman.
"Do you know why these things are
happening?"

"We tried to tell you last night," Venkman
replied.

"Look, mister," Hardemeyer interrupted,
"I don't know what this stuff is or how you
got it all over the museum, but you better get
it off — and I mean right now!"

And as he said this, Hardemeyer pounded
the wall with his fist — and was sucked right
through the slime curtain, until only his
shoes could be seen, embedded in the slime.

The mayor was finally convinced. "Okay,"
he told Venkman. "Just tell me what you
need."

CHAPTER 9

The Ghostbusters worked for hours getting her ready. They knew it was their last hope, their only hope, and they wanted to make sure they did it right.

It was night, just a few hours before midnight, when they were finally ready to set out. Stantz plugged the main cable lead into a transformer and called out, "It's all yours, Pete!"

All four of them were standing in the head of the Statue of Liberty. Venkman plugged the speaker cable into a Walkman and gave a downbeat. Immediately, "Higher and Higher" sung by Jackie Wilson boomed from the huge speakers they had installed inside the historic statue.

The statue, filled with mood slime to capture the good vibes from the people of the city, lurched forward. "She's moving!" Stantz cried.

"I've lived in New York all my life and never visited the Statue of Liberty," Winston said, shaking his head. "Now I finally get here, and we're taking her out for a walk!"

"Okay, Libby — let's get it in gear!" Venkman cried.

As spectators cheered wildly, the Ghostbusters guided the statue up the East River and toward the museum.

At Times Square, nearly a million people were jammed shoulder to shoulder waiting the final ten minutes for the ball to drop and the new year to begin. Looking down Broadway, they saw a magnificent sight. Walking

up the street was the Statue of Liberty, with "Higher and Higher" booming from inside her.

"It's working," said Spengler, checking his giga-meter. "The positive G.E.V.'s are climbing!"

"We're almost there, Lib. Step on it!" Venkman shouted over the happy music.

As the statue approached the museum, the people in Times Square began counting down the last ten seconds to midnight. "Ten . . . nine . . . eight . . . seven. . . ."

Inside the museum, an eerie light spread over the painting of Vigo. Janosz busily painted mystical symbols on the baby's chest. Suddenly Vigo spread his arms wide. His upper body began to move forward away from the canvas.

"Soon my life begins!" Vigo cried. "Then woe to the weak. All power to me. The world is mine!"

The baby's body began to glow as Vigo eagerly reached out for it. A dark shadow suddenly fell over the skylight above the studio.

Janosz looked up — and saw the Statue of Liberty glaring down at him!

Kneeling beside the museum, the statue drew back its right arm and smashed the skylight with its torch. As an avalanche of broken glass fell, the Ghostbusters came hurtling down ropes into the studio. Janosz backed away in fear.

Seeing her opportunity, Dana ran forward and snatched her baby from Vigo's grasp.

"Happy New Year!" Venkman shouted.

Vigo bellowed in rage.

Janosz stepped in front of the painting. "You fools!" he cried angrily. "You dare to challenge the power of darkness, the power of Vigo?"

"Oh, Johnny," Venkman sighed, "did *you* back the wrong horse!"

The Ghostbusters raised their slimeblowers and quickly hosed the helpless, sputtering Janosz into a corner.

Then they stepped forward to finish off Vigo. "Vigi, Vigi, Vigi — " Stantz said, shaking his head. "You've been a bad little monkey."

"Say good night now," Winston said, arming his slimeblower.

Moving quickly, Vigo reached out, grabbed Stantz by the neck, and held him in front of him as a shield.

"Don't shoot! You'll hit Ray!" Spengler screamed.

"Do it! Just do it!' Stantz managed to choke out.

Winston fired and hosed both Vigo and Ray with the positive slime. Vigo let out a cry of disbelief, then fell back into the painting. As the Ghostbusters watched, the paint turned to liquid, and melted off the canvas, revealing another painting beneath it.

The Ghostbusters rushed over to Stantz, who was covered in slime, lying completely

motionless. Winston wiped some of the slime off Stantz's face. "Ray — Ray — how do you feel?"

Stantz smiled lovingly. "Groovy. I've never felt better in my life. I love you guys."

"Oh, no," groaned Venkman. "We've got to live with this??" Then he rushed over to hug Dana and the baby. "What is this — a love-in?" he cried happily, picking up the baby.

"I think he likes you," Dana said. "I think I like you, too."

They kissed.

The others helped Janosz to his feet. "What happened?" he asked, looking very dazed. They explained to him that he had been under Vigo's spell. He didn't really understand, but he looked very relieved to be back to normal.

On their way out, they stopped to look at the painting that had been underneath the painting of Vigo. "There's something very familiar about this painting," Winston said.

In the painting, four archangels hovered protectively over a cherubic baby. Strangely enough, the archangels' faces bore an uncanny resemblance to the four Ghostbusters!

Out on the street, they were all greeted by wild cheering and partying. Everyone started to sing "Auld Lang Syne." What a way to start the New Year!

"Am I too late?" Louis cried, just arriving on the scene.

"No, you're right on time," Stantz told him, handing him a bottle of champagne.

Hardemeyer came staggering out of the museum, covered from head to foot in slime. Even he got into the joyous mood and began singing "Auld Lang Syne" with everyone else.

The mayor came running up to the Ghostbusters. "What are we going to do with the Statue of Liberty?" The statue was sprawled on her back in the park behind the museum.

"She's just sleeping it off," Venkman told him.

Stantz handed the mayor a bill for the night's job. The mayor looked at it and went as white as a ghost! "What? This is way too much! We won't pay!"

Venkman gestured to the statue. "Well, I guess she looks pretty good here in the park, don't you?"

"A lot easier to get to than that island," Stantz agreed.

"Okay, okay!" The mayor knew when he was licked. "If you can wait until Monday, I'll issue you a check."

"Sorry," Spengler told him. "No checks. Company policy."

* * *

A few weeks later, the Statue of Liberty was back on her pedestal, where she belonged. The mayor held a ceremony to celebrate her return. The Ghostbusters and their friends were there as honored guests.

"Pretty impressive, huh?" Venkman said, looking up at the majestic statue.

"It's probably the first thing my grandparents saw when they came to this country," Spengler said.

"From where — Neptune?" Venkman asked.

They all looked up at the statue — just in time to see Slimer fly triumphantly out of one of the windows in her crown. Up Slimer flew, up over the harbor, over the sparkling city, over the shining ocean waters.

It was a beautiful day for everyone — even ghosts.